Gambit

The Broken Bows, Volume 4

Kerri Ann

Published by Kerri Ann, 2019.

This is a work of fiction. Similarities to real people, places, or events are entirely coincidental.

GAMBIT

First edition. July 8, 2019.

Copyright © 2019 Kerri Ann.

ISBN: 979-8227572707

Written by Kerri Ann.

Also by Kerri Ann

Broken Bows, SoCal Soulless MC
Queen
Knight

The Broken Bows
Rook
King
Pawn
Gambit
Bishop's Play

Watch for more at https://www.authorkerriann.com.

Chapter One

"That's enough fucking tinsel!" Jesus fuckin' hell, I've never seen so much bling.

Waving me off, as if it's common knowledge that tinsel is life, Obi continues on, slinging it over the decorative handlebars on the wall. "It's nowhere near enough. Stop whining. I have so much more to do to this clubhouse that the tinsel will be the smallest thing for you to worry about."

Crossing my arms across my chest, I stare down at Obi, grinding my teeth. "Obi, no more tinsel. No more red lights and holly. No more dancing snowmen to the tune of "Rockin' Around the Christmas Tree," and no more presents. We don't do Christmas here."

She gives me the fakest pout I've ever seen, then quickly turns it into a sneaky smile. Placing her hand on my chest, she pinches my nipple. "Lucius, Lu, Luci...come on. You need to let this happen. I won't stop until you relent."

Fuck. When she uses my name instead of my road name at the clubhouse, it makes my cock grow harder.

The wheels start spinning, wondering where in this damn club I haven't taken her yet. There aren't many. We've already worked out our frustrations in the common area, church, and the simple apartment I use when I'm here. That doesn't leave much...

The garage.

I could work with that bench. Letting my mind wander and my imagination process the thought of her bent over that workbench, I *almost* want to yield to her whims on the tinsel. Then again, maybe I'll fight her so she'll yield to me.

I want her to submit.

With Obi standing on the foot stool, tossing tinsel in the air, I swing up behind her. Grabbing her around the waist, I growl, "Time to go."

Throwing her tiny frame across my shoulder. Holding her by the ass, I place my fingers near her core and press against the jeans.

"Hell no, I have things to do. There's a whole box full of decorations needing a place on the walls, Busta." As I rub the material, Obi's protests stop.

Pushing the door open, I step into the sunlight of a warm December in Cali, heading toward the workshop. I doubt anyone will be there. The majority of the club's members are out buying up their last-minute Christmas shit. It's two days until the so-called fat bastard slings his ass down some chimney like he's trying to fit into skinny jeans.

I never had a great relationship with Christmas or any other holiday, at least not since leaving my childhood behind. The DEA didn't exactly treat me like a coddled son. I never had presents left under the tree. There were no fucking cookies laid out, and I sure as shit didn't stay up waiting for Santa. It wasn't my life. When I wanted something, I stole or bought it myself. I didn't wait for some fucking birthday or holiday to surprise myself with a package I'd already bought, and I sure as hell didn't wrap it. Where's the surprise in that?

But unwrapping Oubliette is always a surprise. Each time feels like the first.

Walking across the tarmac, I remind myself that it's only been a few months with this woman. I wasn't sure if a relationship would happen after all the excitement and craziness ended. If after I'd saved her, returned her to her old life and me to mine, that we would be here now, together. She's since put her condo on the market and moved into my place out at the lake. We spend time together like we've been together for years. I guess when you've been through some really bad shit together, it forms a bond, making things—well, easy.

"Where are you taking me, Lucius?" she asks, running her hands down my backside. Propping herself up so that she's upright against me, I lower her body until we're face to face.

Kissing me on the nose, she huffs. "The garage? Really? The dark and dingy garage full of bike bits and trash?"

"Hey, there's no trash in there. Just because the bike's apart, doesn't mean it's useless and ready for the bin."

"Fine. It's not all useless. But I'm sure there's junk in there too. Men always keep things they *think* they'll need in the future."

"Like women and shoes?" I joke, setting her on the seat of an empty framed bike. This is Diesel's ride. Since his crash awhile back, we've been restoring it. I'd helped his dad tear it down last week. We stripped it, sent it out for paint and re-chroming, and we'll be re-installing it all once it's back. For now, it's on blocks. An empty shell with only the recovered leather seat. "Stay," I command.

"No."

Moving to rise up, I bark back, "Obi. Stay put for one second, woman."

Smiling, she wiggles her ass. "Like this you mean? Don't move here? Or here?"

"For Christmas, you'd think I'd been a good enough boy this year to get a woman who obeys." While I shift around some parts at the back, she stands still. Finally. Working away, I know under the stack of shit piled there, there's a saddle. A full-blown horse saddle. One of the older members, Reign, from a time before me, had purchased a ratty saddle on the cheap, wanting to practice his leather tooling skills on it. Eventually, he learned to cut the harsh leather too. Reign's touch is still seen in quite a few of the bikes. From the passed down seats, saddlebags, and vests, I knew he'd even recovered a couch. Seeing it resting in the corner, with boxes stacked on it, I get an idea.

Pushing everything to the side, setting the chrome headlights and whatnots onto another surface, I tap the leather. With dust rising, I brush it off with a cloth.

"C'mere woman."

Her cheeky smile shows her defiance. "Why? Why am I going to sit on a fainting couch?"

"What?" What the fuck is a fainting couch?

Stepping over to me, she pauses in front of me. "It's a beautiful thing, but why should I?"

Working the button on her jeans, I slide my hand down the front until I hit the heated core I'm looking for. "Because I have ideas for this couch. You'll be fainting for sure."

She giggles. That is until I rub the soft spot that flips her switch. Her laugh turns to a cute as fuck groan.

"The guys will be looking for you," she protests. I twirl and tease her body as I push her jeans lower. "We're in broad daylight, standing in the middle of the workshop, Lucius."

"Don't care, Obi." Shoving her jeans all the way down, I've tied up her feet with the material. Pulling up her tiny T-shirt, I drag the bra low and mouth her sweet buds—one, and then the other. Looking up at her face, seeing her melting under my touch, I move closer until her legs are against the edge of the couch. Laying her low, covering her body with mine, I make my way down her milky white skin. Pressing my mouth to her clit, she squeals out in delight.

"Fuck!" Gripping my ears, she shoves me closer still, like she has to force me. "Mmm, so good. Oh, Lucius...oh!" she cries out. I love it.

With a finger within her, hooking it around to the spot I know drives her wild, Obi's warm cunt tightens. I don't want her to come yet; I want her tightness squeezing my cock. Lifting my mouth from her body when I feel her end nearing, I remove my finger and rise above her, wiping her wetness from my lips.

"What the fuck are you doing! Get back down there and finish the job!" she yells, smacking me on the arm.

"I've thought of this all day." Releasing my cock from its confines, I slide inside her tight body. Seeing her up on the ladder, tilting to the side so that I could see up her top as she reached for a spot, or when her jeans rode low and I could see the crest of her ass, made me hard all day.

The feeling of her warm cunt is everything. It's what had me hooked to her those first few times we'd been together. Her pussy is a fuckin' aphrodisiac. Rocking within her, the tight heat squeezes me and my mind clears of everything else. Nothing else matters.

Sanity is overrated when you find the right pussy. I never believed it, thinking it would never happen to me, but it did. Her body fits me like a glove. Her strength, her fire, her attitude, were exactly what I needed in the sack.

I didn't know I'd been a walking fucking corpse of bones, loving nothing and no one. I'm alive and free of King—his machinations—all because of her. I may not admit it to her face, but it's the truth. I may not say it yet, but it's the truth. I handed her my patch within days of meeting her. She understands the intentions of that. Obi knows I won't let her go. Ever.

Thrusting within her, punishing that tight heat to accept more of me—allowing me more time to appreciate the perfection of her body—I pinch her nipples. "Hold out for me. Don't let go, Oubliette." Placing her hogtied legs around my shoulders, feeling my body crest, I hold out just a touch longer, waiting for her to fall apart.

"More. Pump harder! Faster, Lucius!" Her voice always gets hoarse when she's excited. I appreciate what she went through, and no matter what, that little croak reminds me every time. A constant jab for what she almost endured. For what I almost allowed. It makes me appreciate her more. I appreciate that she forgave me and trusted me with her life, her body, and her heart.

Screaming out her release, cresting so hard that her tightness nearly shoves me out, I let go, joining her on the high of our orgasms. It doesn't always happen, but I'll fucking accept when it does.

Thrusting my hips a few more times, trying to make it last, I collapse onto my elbows above her. Leaving a sweet kiss on her nose, I then press my lips to her supple ones. Pushing away the hair from her face, I inhale the sweet smell of her shampoo. That shit makes me wild. I think she uses it just to get me in the mood. It smells like apples in the bottle, but like honey on her.

"You're sniffing my head again," she says, giggling.

"You make me want a PB & Honey. I can't deny you smell amazing."

Kissing my lips again, she grins. "I'll make you one if you'd like. It's one of my specialties." She's not joking. It's one of the only things this girl can make. When it comes to cooking, she's no pro. But the way the peanut butter hits the edge and doesn't goo out, I have to give her props.

If she could only boil water or cook a steak.

Lifting off the couch, zipping my jeans and helping her upright, she pulls her jeans back up. "That was a nice afternoon break, Lucius, but I have to finish the decorations."

"The fuck you do. It already looks like Santa's fucking workshop in there."

"For a man that's never had Christmas, I'm making sure you get the whole experience." Rising up on her tiptoes, she kisses my nose and gives me a wink, then she's off and gone to do God knows what else.

As I'm left standing in the garage, alone, looking at the mess lying around, and without meaning to, Obi has left me with a job.

I don't do the present buying thing. I've never done it, not even for a woman, so I'd fuck that up. But I can build stuff. Seeing materials that would create something she'd appreciate, I set about building it.

Chapter Two

Yanking off my cut, I set it on a hook by the bay door. Rolling up the sleeves of my shirt, I get to work on stacking parts, arranging shelves, shifting fenders, tanks, throttles, and whatever else I find. A few hours later, I'm sweeping the floor of the shop. No one's been in here in a while.

Cruising through a stack of old newspaper clippings shoved in the corner, a picture catches my eye.

The Good Bikers, the title says.

'Willing to always lend a hand, the Broken Bows MC is one of the largest supporters of Toys for Tots in the greater LA area. Their leader, Quint, stated it eloquently: "We're not here to cause trouble. We're here to show the children of this area that bikers can be friendly, approachable, and conscious of the community. My two young boys are here today, helping us collect toys."'

With Quint, Bracken, and Kyden in the picture, the shining example of family values on the cover story, their smiles say it all. There was a time they were happy together. I look at the date: 1998. They were no more than punk kids. Teenagers at most. Whenever things went wrong, it was long before I'd met any of them.

"Hey, Busta. Whatcha doin' in here, man?" Flight hollers, popping his head inside the door.

"Hey." Setting the article back in the box, I grab up a rag. "Cleaning up. Wanna help me out?"

"Fuck no. The ladies have me doin' some shit shopping for fucking turkeys. Something about unstuffed birds. I don't get it." With a wiggle of his eyebrows, his light brown eyes sparkle with mischief. The young idiot is trouble. "I wanna go stuff...*the bird*...if you get my drift."

Yeah. I get him.

"Fine. But send out a prospect to help me at least."

"Sure, Pres," he laughs, walking away.

Twenty minutes pass and three boxes of Harley parts later, I've sorted out what I need for Oubliette's gift. I've never gone shopping for something, so this feels more me. Hand built, with care and consideration, a present from the heart that I know she'll appreciate.

"Pres? Flight said you needed some help." Fletch and Slam, the prospect twins, stand in the doorway like broken images of the last set of twins to grace this place. They've probably never touched a broken bike, only rode what was pristine and in perfect working order. I grew up on the busted. With my dad, Hector—the cunt—the memories of him when he was loving, that's what drives me to be better. The man we know now, the deceased cartel boss, that's the man I'll never be.

"Yeah. Those boxes over there, I need you to load them in the truck and take them to the dump. These here," I point to the one's stuffed to the brim beside me, "take over to Curse's shop. It'll replace the one's we needed last week that he gave us out of his own stock." I pick up the box with the parts I need for Obi's gift, and the newspaper articles. "The rest you can you sort out and shelve it. We're back in the repair business."

"That's awesome," Fletch states, quite exuberantly. "I love fixing shit. Same as Slam. We grew up fixing trash bikes."

Setting the box down, I turn. "You did?"

"Yeah," Slam answers. "Our dad had a shop in Fresno. Didn't True ever tell you that? I mean, that was why we were prospected in. He knew what we could do."

Fuck. Why did True keep so much close to the breast? We could've been way better off if he didn't play things his way—his dad's way.

"Show me what you can do. Start working on that bike over there." I point to Diesel's wreck, knowing there's not much they can do to harm it in the state it's in. Giving them a chance is what's right. "Don't mess with the custom stuff, but the general electrical, re-installation and shit, do that."

With a bright smile showering his face, Slam nearly squeals with delight. "You got it, Pres. We won't let you down."

Feeling good about the boys in the shop, and the gift for Obi, I start for the door of the compound, just as my phone rings. It's my brother, Codero. I love seeing his name pop up on my phone. I know he had the funeral for Rap today, his VP, and when I'd called to see if he'd like us to ride along, he never answered. I've been a bit worried.

"Cap. What's up, man?"

"I need help," he croaks out.

Setting the box down inside the door, I look at Miss and mouth, "Don't touch that" before I answer Cap. "Anything. Where are you?"

"I'm at my club. I'm in trouble."

"I'll be right there."

Chapter Three

Arriving to my brother's clubhouse two days ago, he and I tried to work out the logistics of the situation he was in.

He told me to find him at his garage, a small lean-to off the side of the main house. There were no guards at the gates, none at the door, no men in the yard, and no one to ask me what the fuck I was doing on their property. That alone was fucking strange. Either Cap knew this, or he'd been going lighter on the security. That bothered me.

"Why are we meeting out here? What's up?" I asked as I walked in. That was until I saw him covered in blood. Assuming the worst, I inquired, "That yours?"

"Come on in. I got somethin' to show you."

Leading me to his room at the compound from the outside, instead of through the club, while nearly decapitating myself on the window, the dead woman and the destruction to his room was disturbing. It was a mess. When he'd handed me the card, I knew it spelled danger for us all.

I thought we were done with King and his fucking antics, that it had ended. With the dirty cops, the cartel, our father's demise, I'd assumed we were done with it all. That we could get on with our lives.

I was wrong. We all were.

Taking the bottle that might've been tampered with, and the glass, I'd left. I tried to talk Codero into leaving with me and leaving his club in his taillights, but he swore he'd be safe there.

How wrong he was. How wrong we both were.

It's been two days now since that call. Two days since we'd spoken. Two days that I haven't heard from him. I'm fucking worried. We hadn't been close for years—thanks to our family and the DEA—but after the shitstorm with our father, the death of his best friend Rap, and all points in between, it leaves me uneasy with his radio silence.

Being a few days before Christmas, I'm itchin' to take a ride out.

"Miss!" I call out across the common room of our club. He's been sitting at the bar for over an hour. He and Obi were pouring over gift ideas for the kids of the club, and joke presents for the boys. Right now, he's eyeballing the shot glass that Obi has placed in front of him. It's purple, and aflame.

"One sec." Blowing out the flames, he downs the contents and pushes the notebook they'd been working in with a wink. Setting the glass on the bar and starting toward me, he calls over his shoulder to her, "Nice Tits!"

With a questionable gaze, I track his movements. Wiping his smiling mouth, Miss tosses his hands up in defeat. His response is perfect. "Don't even ask her what the last one was called, Pres."

"Obi and the names for those shots she concocts. I swear she's gonna fucking kill me slowly." Walking out the doors, the two of us exit the clubhouse.

Once we're alone, he asks, "Any news from Johnson on that glass and bottle?"

Rubbing at my beard, I check my messages again. "Nah, man. Still no answer." Pocketing my phone, I add, "I might need to drive over and see him. Being the holidays, though, he's probably with family. I'll give him a call later."

"So what's the problem then, boss?" he questions as we walk toward the bikes.

"It's this fucking present thing. I've never done Christmas. I'm worried."

"Why worry? She's gonna love whatever you've got planned."

Over the top, but I hope she loves it. "You don't think she'd rather have jewelry?"

"Yeah, she will." Stopping, he turns my way. "But what woman doesn't?"

"So what're we doin'?"

"Got an idea. Feel like riding to the rectory?"

He smirks. "Yeah, I'm in." Straddling his bike, he starts it up. "Meet you there in a minute. I need smokes."

Watching as he pulls out of the yard, I give Codero another call. *'This is Cap. If you're a woman, leave your dimensions and number at the tone.'*

"Code, it's me, man. I'm starting to worry about you. I don't want to run to your club, but I will if you don't answer me back in the next few hours."

Fuck.

Last thing I want to do is interfere with his shit, but when I left, I knew it was bad for him to stick around at his club. For him to stay where someone is setting him up, I knew it was a fucking mistake.

"Why are you pacing a dent in the pavement?" Obi asks.

Turning, I grin as she saunters over. "Babe, you need to find better names for your drinks. Nice Tits?"

Laughing, "Come on. With Sex on the Beach and all the other great shot names taken up, I have to come up with original handles that the guys will want to say."

Kissing her on the forehead, petting that flyaway blonde hair down, I tuck her close to my chest. The scent of this woman is an aphrodisiac. Even standing here in full view of the club, I hide my hard-on against her body.

"Is that a gun in your pocket?" She looks up at me and wiggles her eyebrows.

"Funny." Kissing her, tucking my cock to the side, I back away. "Me and Miss are popping out for a run. You'll be good here?"

"Sure. If I need anything, I can ask one of the prospects to take me shopping."

"No more shopping." I straddle my bike. "These kids have never seen anything the likes of what you're doing as it is. You'll have to step up your game next year if you keep this up."

"Next year, huh?" Crossing her arms in mock annoyance, she narrows her eyes and tries her best to look pissy. It isn't working.

Starting the bike, I talk over the rumble of the exhaust. "You took the patch. You're not going anywhere now, Oubliette." She still hates when I call her by her full name. The make-up sex more than pays for it.

Moving away from her and heading out of the clubhouse, I start toward the rectory. After that, I'm going to the Souless clubhouse. I need answers. I know I said I'd pop by in a few hours if I hadn't heard, but something is niggling in the back of my mind. Something's wrong, I know it.

Chapter Four

A s Lucius heads out of the yard and down the street, I turn around and head back to the clubhouse.

I thought he'd never leave.

Standing by the door, waiting for me with a bag full of ribbons and bows, Sinew taps his boot on the floor. "What the fuck took you so long to get him out of here?"

"That man will be the death of me. I swear, I'm not sure I can get this done with only two days left." Grabbing my keys off the wall, Sinew hands the bag to one of the old ladies I just met, Victory's wife, Carol. She's sweet. She's funny. She knows how to drink. "You sure you've got this, Carol?"

"Of course I do. What kind of old lady would I be if I couldn't get this done? Wrangling bikers to do my bidding is a snap." I know she means her husband and son. Victory and Quiver bend over like a handful of straws to that woman's whims. "Don't worry, lady. I've got you covered."

With that comment, I shudder slightly. She doesn't fully understand my issue of loss. That I've lost my parents, almost lost my brother, watched as Panna died, and was unwittingly the instrument in the demise of Nock.

The scars run deep.

I'm leery of making friends in the club. After the fiasco with Scarlet and her blatant murder of Panna, I wasn't sure I could find the heart to like another person. Everyone dies that I love or like.

Lucius and I have talked about my fear of losing him, as well as making another friend and losing them. Everything that's been touched by me has touched me in turn. I don't think I could lose another. It's disheartening. Panna was my only friend here, and I had to watch her die in my arms.

Shaking off the sadness, I try to smile and think of better times as I start for the door behind Sinew. I'd swear he's more excited than I am, and I can't wait to go grab these presents. The one for Lucius especially.

"Which store first? You know how much I hate that big box store for the crowds, so if we can avoid it all together, I'd appreciate it." Popping the door to the truck, he hops inside.

Belting myself in, I close my door. "I hate to break it to you, Buster, but I gotta go there."

He rolls his eyes and whines, "Fine. But you're getting me one of those froufrou coffees."

I smile. "Deal."

"Remember, it has to say dark roast, double shot on the outside. I don't want no one knowin' I'm grabbing something with pumpkin in it." Grinding his hand around the wheel, he chews the inside of his lip where his ring sits.

"Got it. Pumpkin spice, with whip, of course."

Starting the truck out of the lot and down the street, he murmurs, "Pumpkin without whip is a mistake."

Sinew has slowly become one of my favorites, and he's so close to being patched in. If I had a choice, he already would be. I like the kid. He has light brown eyes and caramel skin, with not a scar on his face. He has a post at his eye, a ring in his lip, and I know there's one in his tongue. He's joked there's more, but I'm not up for finding out where. He's clean shaven, head and all, quick with a smile and a joke, and always out to help. If I had a little sister, I'd be trying to set her up with him. Jazzy is the closest to family I have, and there's no way I'd even attempt to set her up with anyone. If Lucius thinks I'm stubborn and unruly, I know he *knows* that Jazzy is worse. He met his match with her. Anyone who meets her does. Jazzy would clean Sinew's clock and send him back to his momma with a bow and a letter of condolences.

Sure, Sinew can hold his own, but Jazzy is a different page in the story. She's nuts. I think that if she finds a man that can match her in wits, antics, and sarcasm—not to mention her riding skills—it'll be a damn fucking miracle. That's why I'm so excited about her present too.

Rounding the street, the outdoor mall is fucking packed. There's not one parking spot. There's a security guard directing traffic, but he's not doing so well, seeing the angry shoppers yelling at him.

I turn to Sinew. "Think you can handle walking a bit? I know a lot we can park at that would be less of a headache."

Wide-eyed, staring at the security guard, I think he feels sorry for the dude. "Anything's better than this hell."

Directing him to a parking lot that's half full of junkers, I see his disproval. "Really? You want me to park here with Busta's truck? You fuckin' mad?"

"Possibly. The verdict's still out."

"I wish you good luck when we get back," he deadpans as he parks beside a rusted, dented, and tireless car.

I can't help but giggle. "Why? Because you're afraid we'll be looking at a disaster when it comes to picking the truck back up?"

Tossing the truck in park, he removes the key from the ignition and turns my way. "No. I'm just glad it's not me telling Busta you lost his truck."

Hopping out, I close the door and start toward the mall with a smile. "Oh ye of little faith. I'll bet you that froufrou drink name on the side of your pumpkin latte that it will be just fine."

"That's a bet I'll take. But only if you're the one explaining to Busta why we took a taxi home."

Rounding the buildings, passing the worn-out looking security guard, we pass through the packed parking lot. The interior of the mall is no less packed with children running around, screaming, and parents rushing with gift-filled arms, wrapped and not. The building is near capacity.

I know exactly where we need to go, and as I make a beeline for it, with Sinew directly on my heels, the shoppers who don't have their heads stuck in cell phone screens jump to the side as we pass through. Something about a big, assuming, black biker in an MC cut does that. When I'm in public with Lucius it's ten times worse. His size, his unapproachable look, it causes the crowds to part. Kids are different. The little boys look up in awe and the girls smile at me with a sense of wonder.

Parents rush around us, but I don't really care. I've been around bikers so long now that I know they at least have a code they adhere to. Regular folks will lie to your face, cheat you out of something to get ahead, and they'll say nice things even when they feel you're worth less than them. Bikers, they see everyone as an equal. One family working toward the same goals. Blood isn't as strong as their care for one another. Strike may have gone outside that, capturing and nearly selling Jazzy and I, but I know that's not the norm.

"Can we just get this over with? I'm feelin' a bit itchy," Sinew groans as he weaves through the crowd. He's moved from behind me and is now in front, probably figuring we'd get a rush on things quicker with him at the helm.

I laugh to myself. "Yeah, it's already on hold. I won't be long."

Popping into the first store, heading straight to the counter, I break through the crowd and head for the sign that reads 'Online Orders.' The weasely looking youngster behind the counter looks ready to quit. I hand him the slip of paper. "I'm here to pick this up."

Checking out the paperwork, then checking his computer, the kid skips to the back. Returning quickly, he blurts out, "I can't lift that." I look up to Sinew.

"Buster, could you please?" I know he hates me knowing his first name, and despises when I call him that, so it's all the more fun. I blame Quiver. He gave me the rundown on all their real names. Buster, though? That one took the cake.

With a sneer and a "Sure," Sinew and the kid head to the back, leaving me to be jostled by the ensuing crowds. I find people watching fun. I like to make up stories about them, about their lives, and what they're there for. In a place like this, it's not hard to imagine what they came for. And if Sinew thinks this is awful, wait until I take him to the next store. It's not kid approved, and I'm quite satisfied with that. I need Jazzy's present after all. She'll hate me and love me in the same measure.

Leaning against the counter, taking in the arguing and wrestling for position at the counters, I nearly miss the yelling at the entrance of the store. That is, until the first shot rings out.

"Everyone, on the ground!" A second shot bounds off the ceiling. "I'm not asking again. All of you, hit the floor, face to the carpet and hands on your heads! No one will be hurt unless there's a fucking hero here!"

I stand there, stunned, looking like a deer in the headlights, waiting for the oncoming transport.

Moving toward me, the man is masked up with some yellow cartoon character I don't recognize, and a bright blue ball cap. Pointing the gun at me, he yells, "Did you not hear me? Do you not understand to hit the fucking dirt?"

He's so close, I can make out some of his features. It's frightening and electrifying at the same time. My body is so set on fight or flight that I don't move, even as he speaks directly to me. His eyes are an electric blue. There's a small scar under his right eye that I can just see, even with the mask. His lashes are super fucking long.

As I open my mouth to speak, and he moves to touch my shoulder, a loud crash rings out. "What the fuck do you think you're doing, kid!" With a gun raised, pointed at the robber, Sinew has an arm cannon directed just over my shoulder. I can see the barrel of it, and I see this going wrong. I'm the monkey in the middle of an O.K. Corral shootout. While others in the room are sobbing or screaming for their loved ones, I stand still. I don't...I can't.

"I'm giving you one last chance to put down that fucking gun before a bullet leaves mine. You can run out the back door and straight to the street. I don't fuckin' care if you take a stack of TVs with you on the way out, but you best put that fuckin' gun down. I have great aim and no fear of using it." With his Compton accent thick and pissy, Sinew is not about to let some little jackass harm me or anyone else here. "Come on. I'm not known for being one with patience," he releases the safety, "but to make it easy, I'll even step to the side for you."

The gaze from the bright blue-eyed intruder is fully focused down the barrel of the gun in Sinew's hand. The look is that of shock and awe. He's surprised that a guy like Sinew is giving him a chance and offering him a way out.

Not taking his eyes from Sinew, he lowers the gun slightly. Keeping it trained toward us, he sidesteps me, pushes his way around the counter and past the piss scared employee. Hearing his feet hit the floor heavily as he runs toward the rear exit, tells me our would-be robber is in the wind.

Relocking the safety on his gun, removing it from my sight and stuffing it back in his waistband, Sinew asks, "You good?"

I don't speak, but I do pick my jaw back up off the ground. Clearing my throat, all I can say is, "Wow."

"You can get up now. The guy's gone," Sinew states loudly to the room. "Go back to spending all your money. Show how you love someone with a flat screen."

The room scrambles, some running away into the crowded halls of the open mall, some picking up a phone and calling someone who cares. I look at our weasely employee.

"You good?" Sinew asks him.

Pulling off his company logo shirt, he tosses it to the counter. "I'm done. This doesn't pay enough, man. Take whatever the fuck you want."

I snicker. "I'll just take what we came for, thanks."

When the room is more manageable, Sinew gathers up the gift for Diesel and starts toward the door. "You comin'?" he asks me.

"Yeah, but don't you think the cops might want to ask you about this? Shouldn't we stick around to—"

"I'm Clark Kent, not Superman. Let's go." He turns and walks out.

Following him to the truck, I speak up. "That was fucking crazy, Buster. Thank you."

"Does trouble follow you, or do you seek it out?" he huffs while strapping the TV box to the bed of the truck.

"I used to think I was just in its way. Not anymore. I think I'm the divining rod."

Chapter Five

I left the rectory about an hour ago. Miss headed off for some last-minute present shit and I drove over here. This time when I pull up to the gates of SoCal Soulless, there are two guys on watch. One is a prospect, the other a patched member. Odd, as they don't normally get relegated to this kind of shit.

Shutting down my bike as I approach, I let it coast in silently. The first to approach is the patched member. He's a slender guy with a short haircut, his curls tightly knotted. Rolling close, I see that his scruffy, sparse beard are actually areas where no hair grows. Thick scars with pinched skin, poorly repaired, and definitely damaged by heat. I know Cap's boys are mostly ex-military, so I can only assume he was hurt in a firefight. His patch states his road name as Lizard.

Laying down my kickstand, I stay on the seat. "I'm here to see Cap." Lizard looks over my cut, eyeballing it from top to bottom. "Wanna see my fucking ass tattoo too?" Lizard stays quiet, but the prospect snickers.

With a dark glare turning to the prospect, Lizard flicks his gaze back to me. Raising a hand, motioning to the other guy, he starts to sign words.

Nodding his head a few times, responding in turn, the prospect looks my way. "Did he know you were comin' by?"

"Nah. We didn't have a fucking lunch date." I blow out a breath, frustrated by the gatekeepers. "Can you just tell him his brother is here?"

He looks surprised. "Brother? I thought his family was all dead."

"Nope. Just his fucked-up father. Now, tell him I'm here, *prospect*, and open the fucking gates."

The other man signs something before the prospect answers. "He's not here. Went out a while ago."

"Like how long ago?"

"If you're family, wouldn't you know his whereabouts?"

"You always this disrespectful to a fuckin' Pres?" I rise off my bike. "I don't wear this fuckin' rocker as a Halloween costume."

Lizard motions to the prospect, wildly signing, as the other tries to keep up. "You know I can't read that fuckin' fast, Lizard." Slowing his motions, the other man watches intently, then turns back to me. "He left two days ago with Yeti. Target practice with some guy named Trigger. They separated at the club." Turning to the other guy, he questions, "What club again?" Lizard responds. "Right. Humble. Anyway, Yeti left with a girl, and didn't think anything of Cap being gone when he came out of the VIP."

"Yeti here?" I ask, frustrated further.

"Nah. He left yesterday for a ride and hasn't been back."

I knew something was fucking wrong. I knew he should keep his nose clean and stay away from his club until we could figure it out. Now he's missing, and these fucks don't care enough to ride out and find their goddamn Pres.

Containing my anger, I remind myself it's not my club and not my problem to fix their faults. Though when I catch up with my brother, I'll be having a heavy talk with him.

I sit back down and start my ride. "Thanks for the info. If he returns today, tell him to give Busta a ring, yeah?"

Moving away from the curb, riding a ways down the street, I pull over when I'm far enough away. "Fuck. I told you it was bad for you to stick around. I knew. I fucking knew it."

And this Yeti guy? I need to grab some intel on him.

Dialing Cap's phone once more, I again get his voicemail. Disconnecting the call, I immediately call Miss, who picks up on the second ring. "Yeah."

"Something's up. I need a meet with Death. You up for a ride?"

"Not a question. I'll meet you at Humble in ten," he responds before hanging up the phone.

Chapter Six

Handing over the pumpkin drink foaming with thick whip, the smile on Sinew's face is perfection. Licking the topping, he takes a sip. It's just as hilarious to see as you would expect. All six foot six of him melts at the first taste of his drink. He's lucky too. Most of the retailers stop selling it at the first sight of Black Friday sales. This one close to Humble keeps it available until New Year's Day.

With a mustache full of whip, he growls, "You know I have to tell him."

"Shit. I thought the extra-large drink might have changed your mind." Holding the door for him, we head back out to the truck. I could've grabbed the drinks for us, but after the electronics' store attempted heist, he wasn't letting me out of his sight.

The last stop at the sex store, I think short circuited his wires. He asked the sales girl more questions than she's probably ever been asked. Even a couple she had to look up the answers to online. But I'm glad. I got the best present imaginable for Jazzy.

Being this close to work and still on my imposed vacation, I'm itching to touch my bar. We're only three or four doors down, so I figure I can coax Sinew into it. "Mind if we head to Humble for a sec?"

He furrows his brows. "You think you have to ask me if I wanna head to a strip joint after sitting in that sex store for an hour? My cock's so—"

"Fucker! No. Just no, okay. My ears can't handle that. Just don't."

He laughs and sips at his drink with a huge grin, knowing he has the upper hand. The last thing I want to know is what he intends to do with that strap-on dildo. Who and what it's for is way past my imagination.

Crossing the street, as we're about to enter the club, I hear the distinct sound of rumbling bikes. Turning to look before we head inside, I'm surprised. It's Lucius and Miss.

"Guess they had the same idea," Sinew cackles.

I round on him. "Not a word. Not a word about today or I'll tell them what you were looking at in the sex store."

His eyes bug out before he narrows his sights on me. "You wouldn't blackmail me."

I point to his cup—the one that says 'pumpkin' on it—as a reminder that the truck was still there. I'll play all my cards if it keeps me out of trouble. "Call it a professional courtesy if we both just kept our mouths shut."

As the two bikes corner the building to park out back, Sinew opens the front door of Humble for me. "You're a bad woman, Oubliette. Perfect for the Pres." He mumbles the rest, something about me being designed by the devil. Enjoying it, I smile and pass him by.

Stepping up the front stairs, Sinew pulls off his cut as the two of us enter my work. Saying hi to Axel—the security for today—we walk through the heavy crushed velvet purple curtain, where the sounds and sights are heavenly. Man. I can't express how much I missed this shit.

At the top of the stairs, Apoc's chatting up a young, cheap stripper named Sassy. I like her, I just don't *like* her for Apoc. I've told them both that more than once. He's better than that cheap perfumed piece of ass.

"Sassy. Don't you think it would be better to find a paying customer?" I ask, tapping her on the shoulder.

As she turns my way, smirking and licking her upper lip like it's a lollipop, her cheap smile is as fake as her lashes. "Apoc's good company."

"You mean, a good "in" to his brother." It's not a lie. Apoc's young, only turned twenty-two and not patched. If he keeps it up, it won't be long, but for now he's not worth her trying to claw her way to the top.

"I could use some company," Sinew pipes up.

Sassy gives him a once-over before pawing the front of his jeans. With a look I could only consider shock, she smiles wide. "Come with me, puddin.'"

Taking a big gulp of his drink, he hands his cup to me. "Don't throw this out. I'll reheat it in a few."

I snicker and snort. If he only needs a few, then Sassy won't be so happy. With a quick smack to the shoulder, Sinew smiles and hustles off to the VIP area.

As the two of them leave, I turn to Apoc with a roll of my eyes.

"Missed you, O." Pulling me in for a hug, I accept it gladly.

"Missed you too, kid," I say into his chest.

With the vibration of the song currently playing in the club rumbling across him, I almost miss his soft, "I'm sorry."

He's still thinking it's his fault that I was taken. That I should've been at the club and secured. That no one should've touched what they consider family. I've watched Apoc grow up, changing from a thin waif of a kid, scrawny and spilling for a fight, into a man that's as full—if not as big, possibly bigger—than Death.

As I pull out of his embrace, I see the conflict in his deep brown eyes. He's gorgeous, and becoming more stunning every second. His long hair is pulled tight into a thick braid at the back, with loose bits framing his model perfect face. No wonder the whores chase his ass around. Still, I feel obligated to keep him out of shit. He's the closest I have to a little brother, and I won't let anyone turn him into a broken man.

"I hear your man's popping by for a sit with Death. You here for that reason?" he asks with a simple smile.

"Nah, I didn't know he was coming by. Actually, I didn't know *I* was coming by. It's a fluke we're here together." Seeing Lucius walk through the back door, his stern face of concern has changed to surprise. He must have really had something on his mind. That hard gaze I've seen a few times now, that I don't wish to be on the receiving end of ever again, is firmly in place. His mind is elsewhere, worrying about something pretty heavy.

Talking to Miss quickly, he walks my way. I watch the way his body moves, the way his whole demeanor changes when he relaxes. When he's mine.

"Babe. What are you doin' here?"

I give him a wicked smile. "I was shopping, and had a need to feel my bar. I missed it."

"Who's with you? Who's watching you? You know I said you go nowhere without protection, right?" His comment is sweet, but with an undertone of worry.

"Sinew's in the back. We just got here. Didn't you see us when you passed the front door?" It's like I'm a total shock to his serious thoughts.

He shakes his head. "No, babe, I didn't see you. But I'm glad you're with Sinew. At least he'll keep you out of trouble."

I smile, knowing that was almost a no. I know that right now, wherever his thoughts are, it wasn't on his surroundings as he passed me. Rising up on my tiptoes, I kiss him. "I have a thing with Death that we need to go over. You'll stay here and wait for Sinew, right? No walking out the back?"

Funny, not so much.

"Yeah, I'm good. I want to go hug my bar and remind it that I love it. I think it's feeling lonely."

Taking my hand, he places it over his crotch. "You're a funny girl, Obi." Stepping back, he grins. "Go pet your bar. But remember, I'm the only wood you're stroking."

"Deal." With that, he kisses me on the forehead and walks off to find Death and Miss.

Chapter Seven

Telling Death about my concerns with Cap—his disappearance here at the club, or shortly after—we decide to check out the video footage.

"Sure, he was here the other day. I saw him come in. Him and Trigger went out for a bit of target practice. When they came back, his SA went to the VIP, and when I saw him last, Cap was hanging with my sister over there." Pointing to the screen that shows the current couple seated where he once was in the feed. "I'll go back to Tuesday and we'll see where he went."

Clicking a few buttons, changing the time and date, Death moves the system back until Cap and Jasmine are sitting on the seat. The two of them are enjoying a few drinks, chatting it up, then twenty minutes in, Cap walks off. "Hang on. Let me change to another frame." Clicking away, Cap is seen walking across the bar area, past the employee only area, then off screen again.

"Fuck. Where the hell is he going?" I ask.

I'm frustrated. Trying to figure out where he's gone is even more of a mystery when he disappears in a place like this. There are enough cameras here and angles to showcase every tit, slung dong, and piece of ass imaginable.

"I'll bet he's gone out for a smoke. The employees will go out through the employee only exit instead of out the side door for clients. It's a bit quieter. Jaz probably told him to go out that way," Death offers, flicking the screen to the back exit that heads to the bikes. It's the same door that Oubliette went out. It's the same one where she was taken.

Fucking irony can kiss my ass.

As Cap ventures off screen and out the back door, my worst fears are confirmed. There are two men dressed in gaudy fucking shirts, the stench of *Chicano* wafting off of them.

"Who the fuck are they? And why are they here?" Miss questions.

"No idea."

Cap is having a calm conversation with the guys at first, and then he's shot by what seems to be tranquilizer guns. I watch as he slumps to the ground. With a boot to his side, the guy checks to see that Cap's out, then they load him in an SUV and leave.

"Can you get a plate off that?" I ask Death.

Shaking his head, he turns around in the chair. "Nah, the angle's wrong. But we might be able to get more info from my buddy at the sheriff's department. He owes me one anyway."

"I can check with the DEA. They look like guys they might be keeping tabs on." I didn't recognize either of the fuckers, so that leaves us at a disadvantage.

"Can you send me a copy of that?"

"Yeah. I'll text it to you."

Me and Miss leave the security room and head toward the exit door. Stepping out, the sun is setting, and the Cali heat is still scorching hot. "Fuck me, it's hot out here," Miss groans, pulling at his shirt.

Ignoring him, walking down the staircase, I turn to the spot that the camera noted Cap had been. Checking the ground and surrounding area, I find exactly what I'd expected. Another fucking Queen playing card.

Who the fuck is this Queen?

Showing it to Death, he shrugs. Miss does the same. We're at a loss to this. I'd left the first card with Cap back in his room at the compound, so I decide to take this to the DEA contact I have, along with the picture of the two assholes that took my brother.

"I gotta get a handle on this. It's fucking nuts that we're going through this with another fucker player." Stepping back up the stairs, heading back to the club floor, the sound of the booming bass is almost overpowering. I'm revving for a fight, and a loud song isn't slowing my heart rate.

"There's not much you can do right now, Busta. Most fuckers are on holiday. You might have to wait."

Passing the bar chairs, packed to the gills with boys from his club, Death sends me a grin with a chin raise. He asks, looking at Obi, "She driving you nuts about Christmas bullshit? She used to drive me batshit crazy."

That's hitting the fucking nail on the head. "Fucking woman is a Christmas nightmare. I've never done this and she's killin' me."

"Never done what?" Death asks jokingly.

"Christmas. You don't do that shit in DEA fucking care. King didn't treat us like his kids, he treated us like instruments. I figured out fast that no one buys you a fucking present unless you buy it yourself," I tell him as we walk up to the bar.

Talking over the music, Death smirks. "That's deep, Scrooge. Good luck on passing that by her, though. She's a fucking lunatic for Christmas. Her not on shift here for a few weeks has given us a reprieve this year. I think the dancers are appreciating it."

"Well, she's made up for it in our club and my house. I drew the line in the fucking sand on dressing up my bike. There was no way she was tossing blinking lights and tinsel on it." I look directly at the mastermind of Christmas hell behind the bar, shaking, pouring, frothing and measuring out shots on the bar. By the looks of it, I'd say she's poured Perky Nipples. The gang of onlookers patiently waiting on their insane shot glasses is hysterical.

With a silly *"Ooh!"* Miss jumps ahead of Death and I, making a beeline for the rail.

"Good fucking Lord!" Her and those concoctions have cost me and our bar a rise in liquor prices. Laughing it off as the bright hued drinks are poured, the moment reminds me of her gift.

"I got something to take care of," I tell Death. "I'll be right back."

Acknowledging me with a smile, I look back at Obi and Miss. I won't worry about either of them for the moment. They'll look after one another. Stepping out the front, I dial the number.

"Hey, Lucius. I'll bet your checking on that shit you dropped off."

Mind reader.

"Yeah, I am. How's it goin'? You almost done?" I ask Grady, Oubliette's brother. He's kinda handy with metalwork—a hobby of his—and he's finishing off the present for Oubliette.

"I'll have it ready in an hour. Thank fuck I took off this week or it never would've been done, man."

"I appreciate the rush. I know she'll love it."

"You know she will. I know my sister, she's going to lose her shit with it."

I won't deny that. Smiling as I think of how she'll react—how much head I'll get out of this—I thank him and hang up. I'll head over there later, once I get the truck back from her and Sinew.

Dialing another number, I call my contact handler, the guy they assigned after our fiasco with King. Connecting, he answers. "Fredrick Johnson."

Buddy must not use call display.

"Hey, it's um...Agent Lucius Guierra. I have a question for you pertaining to my father, Hector."

I hear shuffling noises in the background. "Hey, Lucius. Yeah. Sure. I was just packing up for holidays...wife wants to visit family in Florida. Give me what you need."

"I know Magnus liked to leave playing cards as his calling card, the King, but does, or did, anyone else do that?"

The line goes quiet, and I can hear him take a seat. With a sharp intake of breath and a slow release, he responds. "Yeah. He got the idea from his boss when it came to playing out that particular signature. Did you get another one?"

Should I tell him? Fuck. If I need his help and his trust, I should give him a bit. "Yeah. A Queen."

"Shit. That's not good." He pauses, but doesn't elaborate. Nothing like the suspenseful pause before the killer arrives.

I guess I gotta ask to get the info. "Why?"

"Working with Alta Noche, did you have dealings past the bagmen and King?"

Confused, I reply back, "No. Why? Who the fuck's the puppet master?"

"Her name is Claudine Marie Consuela Cruz. She's your father's new wife. She *is* the Queen. She's the largest trafficker of cocaine from central Mexico."

"My father had another wife?" I nearly shout it clear across the street. I'm loud, I know I am. Noticing that it causes the cock sucking asshole accountants and other business motherfuckers in the area to turn and stare at me, I don't apologize. Nothin' to apologize for.

I'm fucking amazed by all the secrets. The fucking twists and near insanity that my family has become is beyond comprehension.

"Yeah. She's a fucking nut case. She makes male cartel bosses seem like wet nurses."

"Johnson, you think you could do me a favor and send me all you have on her, on her whereabouts and shit? I have a feeling she's up to something." With that card at Cap's, and the one here where he was taken, I know for a fact we're in for something fucking huge.

"Did you go pissing in cartel beds again?"

"Possibly, but I can't be certain, Johnson. I gotta ask...this Claudine Cruz, did she know about us? Hector's kids?"

"As far as we know, yes. She's also more than likely found out about your little coup against her cartel and the retaliation against her husband."

"Shit. This is payback then?" I mumble, but loud enough that Fredrick hears me.

"What's payback? Is something going on?"

Fuck me. Deciding to keep quiet, I fudge the truth. "We've just had some dealings, and I'd like to clear it up before I give you further intel. Plus, it's Christmas. Go enjoy time with your family. If I need anything else, I'll wait until after Christmas."

"New Years," he corrects me. "I'm off until the fourth."

Before hanging up, I offer, "Hey, Johnson, if there's a couple bodies at your door on New Year's Day requiring toe tags, thank me afterwards." Hanging up the line, not waiting for his response, I'm surprised when my phone dings immediately.

Opening my mail, seeing the files from Johnson, I thumb through them. I'm still fucking amazed that after everything with Magnus, that anyone at the office even answered my call, let alone gave me the details I needed. I'll consider this my Christmas present from the company I never got anything from before. Nothing but heartache and lonely nights.

Tossing through the attachments—pictures of her, of Hector, and her looking happy, I'm still thrown for a loop. Playing it back in my mind—my life, my family—I think about what my father, Hector, had said about my mother. He'd always acted like she was the love of his life, that she was irreplaceable. I knew she'd died a little while back, but how long ago was not something I knew. Knowing now that Hector had another wife—a psycho cartel lunatic—I think it's best I don't know.

My mother, Diedre Watson, was a crazy strong black woman. She ruled my brother, our sister, the club, and me with a wooden spoon. If our father had found a wife even *more* unruly, then he's pretty fuckin' special. If Hector could marry two of them, or find a way to work with two, then he deserves his own circle in hell for the effort.

"Hey. You 'bout ready to head out?" I hear Miss ask from behind me.

Locking my phone and turning his way, I reply, "Yeah, I'm good. Is Obi still cooking up a storm?"

He grins wickedly. "Fucking hell she is! The Furry Cock Nuggets were tasty." Licking his lips, his face goes serious, with a hint of embarrassment. "Never thought I'd say shit like that. Don't tell anyone, Pres. I have a rep, you know."

Walking on ahead to the bikes, I smirk. "We wouldn't want anyone to think you're a pussy, Miss. Consider your secret safe."

He laughs as he straddles his bike. "I'm gonna pay for this in the long run, ain't I?"

Starting my bike, I lift the kickstand. "Every fucking day."

Chapter Eight

Knowing that I was leaving Humble later than Lucius, Sinew and I took the presents—that I'm hiding—to my brother's house. After unloading, and with a quick kiss hug combo, the two of us returned to the club with an impatient Lucius hanging by the doors.

"Where have you two been? Death told me that you'd left the club hours ago."

We did, but I don't know how to tell him where we were without raising suspicion. I knew he needed the truck, but this was too important to leave. It was necessary.

"We had to take the last present I'd bought for Quiver to the chrome shop. I'd called ahead, and they said it could get done, so I rushed." Raising up on my tiptoes, I kiss him on the cheek. I'm trying to get out of telling him the truth, that the last present was for him. I've already picked up Quiver's chrome set of shot glasses for the bar, and that I was at the Harley store with Sinew. I'd ordered a helmet. It may seem weird to hand him a helmet for Christmas, one that's for me, but I did.

"I'll be back in a bit," he says, hopping into the truck. "We'll go out to dinner, yeah?"

Smiling like an idiot, I say, "I'd love that."

After closing the door, he powers down the passenger window. "I'll be back as quick as I can." With that, he starts the truck and leaves.

I've always been a big giver when it comes to Christmas. I feel itchy when I don't buy presents for everyone. Usually, it's just Grady, Jaz, Apoc, and Death that I buy for, so this year is a big deal.

My parents loved to slather us with gifts, and when it all came to a screeching halt, I made sure that every year was perfect for anyone I cared for. The guys at Lucius' club have never been the giving type. Their old president had moved away from showering others with love. Lucius wanted to change his club, and I figured what better way than to exchange gifts and have presents for the kids. Now that I've spent a small fortune, taped shut more wrapping than I've ever done, I'm complete. It will be a great Christmas. I swear it. Nothing will ruin this if I have a chance to make it amazing.

Chapter Nine

"You're sure? You tried them all out and everything works?" I'm at Grady's house, out in the hills, and his oversized idiot of a dog is rubbing up against me as I try to avoid petting his ass. Kessel, his three-legged Mastiff, was a ward of our club for a month or two, as Grady went in for an experimental cancer treatment in France. *It* fell in love with Radish, Trigger's service dog, and the dumbass animal followed me everywhere. I guess it was my own fault. I walked around with treats in my pocket. Every time he'd head over to Miss and bark loudly, I'd laugh, stick out my hand with a treat, and pet him on the head. He went back to Grady a few pounds heavier.

"I'm sure, I'm sure. I tested them all," he says with a grin, while wrapping the gift in newspapers so nothing gets damaged.

Looking to his girlfriend, Gemma, she smiles too. "They worked great. We had to try them each out, of course. It was a long night."

Great. He's tried them out before she will. I'll never hear the end of this. Obi will harass me for that. Once he has them all wrapped up and settled in a bag that I can lay in the back of the truck, I thank him.

Thinking about the conversation with Johnson earlier, about the cartel and all the shit going down, I'm wondering if Oubliette would be safer with her brother, or with the club if things go down.

"Grady. If Oubliette needs a place to hide out for a bit, will you be around over the holidays?" I know Obi and he normally get together and reminisce about family over the holidays, but with the newest edition of Gemma in her brother's life, I'm not sure if they're going to see her family instead.

"Yeah, I'll be here. Gem's family is coming for a visit tomorrow. It'll be a houseful. It would be weird not to see my sister on a day like this." Suddenly, he looks worried. "Should she be? I mean, staying out here? Is something going down at the club again?"

"Nah. Nothing with us. It's just if something were to happen, I wanted to confirm you'd be around."

Grady knows I'm jerkin' his chain, but he doesn't let on. "Sounds good. Let her know dinner is at four."

Wrapping herself around Grady's midsection, Gemma adds, "And I expect you too." I appreciate the gesture, as she's making sure I know that I'm more than welcome.

Opening the door for the truck, I grin back. "Sounds good. Thanks again for the rush job. I know Obi will love it even more knowing it came from you."

Starting the truck and waving goodbye, I tear off out of suburbia toward the clubhouse. During the drive, I had this niggling feeling of being watched. That someone was tailing me. Though, every time I looked at the cars around me, nothing stood out.

Pulling into the compound, parking and looking at the traffic through the rear view, I waited to see if something did a slow drive by or stopped near the gates. Nothing. Still, I had a sense of unease.

Locking up, I walk to the front doors of the garage. I'm in awe. The floors gleam, the shelves are stacked and neat, and Diesel's bike has the engine half done.

"Well, fuck," I say, thinking I'm all alone.

"Hey, Pres." Popping up from behind the frame covered in oil, grime, and dust, Fletch's smile is so wide, I see his molars.

"Hey," I say. "Where's Slam?"

"Over here." From the back, I hear a door slam against a wall. "Did you know there's a back room?"

"No. Really?"

"Yeah. It's stacked with old bike parts. Even a Captain America tank. It's fucking awesome. It's like a goddamn candy store of Harley." He indicates the room with a nod. "Come see."

Shit. Stepping in, I'm truly amazed. The old man had this garage packed to the brim with boxes and shit. I'd never seen this room. I'd bet only the lifers from Bows might have. There are shelves full. It really is a Harley paradise.

Lifting a wide glide front end and a set of custom ape hangers, his grin is blinding. "There's enough back here to build a whole ride." Setting them lovingly on a wall hanger, the two pieces rest gently against the side. "There's even an old fifty-eight leather Sportster seat and a King Queen seat too. Both are in great condition. Pres, it's gonna take me a week to go through just this room."

I ask the question I'm sure that's burning a hole in his tongue, "Do you and Fletch wanna be the boys back here? The shop boys?"

His eyes go wide and fill with excitement. "Yeah, man. That would be a fucking gift. I'm telling you, we won't let you down on repairs. The two of us will start with your ride if you want. I mean, only if you want." He's nervous, but I'm excited to have someone in our garage again, someone who can bring it back to life.

"No worries with mine right now. Though, I know Quiver needed a bit of help on his. The engine's been giving him a hard time on cold starts."

He's so excited, he looks about ready to pee his pants. I get it, though. I've given him and Fletch a very important task, one that normally isn't given to prospects. Never mind two of them that haven't been here long. Thing is, I trust them. I didn't force them into this, and they seem to be in their element. The shop has been cleaned and rearranged, and Diesel's ride was started, all in an afternoon. They're the right men for the job.

I give him a smack on the shoulder. "You two did good." With a head nod, I motion toward the clubhouse. "Now go see Quiver. Grab the keys to his ride and see if you can get it figured out for him."

"Yes, sir." Running off out of the back room, I hear him talking to Fletch.

Staying in here, admiring the space and the pieces that have been collecting dust, warms my heart. This club is coming together, just like I'd hoped it would.

Now to figure out my brother's whereabouts.

Locking up the back room and walking out, the leather couch is resting by the door. Dusted off, and shined up with conditioner, it calls to be sat on properly. Taking a seat, I start back on the files that Johnson forwarded to me. It's less than two days until Christmas and I'm fucking worried.

Looking at the picture of the Queen, Claudine Cruz, her known associates, and the large 'Deceased' stamped across her husband's picture, I check out the information.

Age: Forty-seven (DOB) April 4th
Height: Five-six (Approx.)
Visible scars: Scar along her neck from an attempt on her life at fifteen. Tattoo on her right wrist of a sparrow.
Family: No dependants. Husband (recently deceased).
Wealth: Unknown. Estimated at one hundred-fifty million (US dollars).
Main trafficking component: Cocaine and human trafficking. Dabbles in Marijuana and Meth production.
Location: Rioverde, Mexico (Estate of fifteen hectares surrounded by mountainous range and rivers). Impassable from the mountains, but accessible through extensive tunnels throughout the area.

The file shows pictures of the estate, her large house, outbuildings and such. There's fencing, and shots showing the locations of cameras, trip systems, land mines, and more guards than I've ever seen. If for some reason she's taken Cap there, we're going to have a hard time getting him out.

That doesn't mean I won't, but it's not going to be a cake walk. As I sit there thumbing through it all, I hardly notice when Obi arrives. "Hey, sexy. Wanna give a girl a ride?" Plunking herself down on my lap, straddling my legs, her knees are up on the couch and her tits are covering the phone I was viewing. I don't mind the change in venue. This is a better view for sure.

Setting my phone on the couch, I turn my attention to her. "I only have eyes for one lady. She'd cut my balls off if I answered yes."

With an airy giggle, Oubliette wraps her arms around my shoulders and pulls me in close for a kiss. I always feel like the beast to her beauty. Mind you, her beauty doesn't end on the inside. She's fucking gorgeous inside and out.

"You're somewhere else," she states, assessing me.

"I won't lie to you. Yeah." I promised her that I wouldn't hide things from her. I can't tell her what goes on in church, but this is outside of that, for now. It's family.

She lifts off my lap and lays on the couch with her legs across mine. "Tell me about it."

Blowing a breath out my nose, I begin. "It's Codero. He's been having a bit of trouble, and now I can't get a hold of him. I think something big is going on." Pulling the card from my pocket, I show her the Queen. "This was left at Humble in the alley where he went missing."

Her body stiffens slightly, but she tries to hide it as she inspects the card. "*The* alley? Like the one that...that alley?"

"Yeah. That one." Taking the card back, I put it inside the inner pocket of my cut. "I don't want it to ruin the holiday, but the boys and I might have to go on a ride."

She starts to chew on the inside of her mouth. "I get it. Are you sure that she has him and where? Like, do you know where to go?"

"Nah, I don't. That's the big issue." Picking up her hand, I turn it over and kiss her palm. "I'm trying to get confirmation before we do anything. It's hard, though."

"You'll open presents no matter what. That's an order. Everyone has worked hard to make this a great new addition to your club. The kids and parents are looking forward to it. It's what families do.

Agreeing with her, I smile. "I'll do my best to have us here for the fat fucker."

She smacks my arm and grins. "I didn't work this hard for you to enjoy Christmas, just for you to mess it up."

"I get ya, lady. I get ya." Moving, I rise. "I think it's time to head home. It's been a long fucking day, and you need sleep so that you can tinsel the fuck out of the rest of this joint."

"Funny. Not so much, mister." Standing with a hand up, she bounces on her toes. "Keep it up, and I'll put lights on that Harley."

"Over my dead fucking body," I laugh, smacking her ass. "Now let's go home. I have a need to fuck something."

Chapter Ten

L ast night was great. I think Lucius wore out his tongue, and I know for sure that sitting on that Harley today, my fucking core hurts. I'm glad the windows at the house were closed or everyone around the lake would've heard me screaming *"Harder, faster! Put your back into it!"*

Today has been nuts. Bustling from the moment we walked through the doors of the clubhouse, I've been helping Carol, Gazie (who's still on the mend after her surgery), Helen, Margo and Bernie with the turkeys. The roomful of women have been stuffing birds, cutting carrots, and drinking wine since seven-thirty this morning. We came in extra early. I know that Lucius is really worried about Cap, but he's trying to avoid leaving with the boys on the day before Christmas. He knows how much this means to me, how badly I want this to go off without a hitch, and that this is important for the club when it comes to rebirth. They wanted new beginnings, and this is the best way to start.

"You're telling me you have no tattoos? You've worked in a biker bar for how many years?" Helen asks. She's a long-standing lady in the club. She's close to Miss, but they've never been formal about their arrangement. She's a nice enough lady, and she's more than willing to assist. She's beautiful too. With thick lush braids down her back, tied back in a bright orange tie, she's stunning. Her striking brown eyes and full lips make me jealous. Also, her arms are covered in ink. Intricate black lines that are characters from her favorite movies. It adds to her beauty.

"I guess I just never got around to it. Not that Jazzy didn't try to talk me into it, it's just that I've never had something that fit me." It's permanent, and I want something that means the world to me. I'd see it every day, so it's got to be special.

"They're permanent, but adjustable. I can say that my first is actually hidden under layers of clothing most days, but that it's a reminder that I've changed. It's still a part of me, but not important like it was then."

Carol starts crying. She's been peeling onions and cutting them up for the stuffing.

"What's it like?" I ask. I'm really curious, but nervous about the pain.

"It's easy. It hurts less than when they bite your nipples. It's just a constant nip is all." Helen winks and smiles. It's my first time hanging out with her, and I feel that Jazzy and Helen would become fast friends. She has a thing for pink wine, and they've been drinking bottle after bottle. At this rate, they'll all be puddles of insanity by the day's end.

I told Lucius that I have a tradition that needs to be upheld, and that today is very important.

When my parents died, Tin—my nickname for my brother Grady—made sure I'd find joy in every day of the holidays. We open our gifts to one another the night before, and the dinner is on Christmas Eve. On Christmas, it's a day of relaxing, junk food, and movies. Pies, pizza, grilled cheese, or whatever crap food we wanted on that day. The night before was ours to dress up, reminisce and celebrate. Lucius is helping to make that happen, bringing in all the club members and their families for one giant party.

Lucius had mentioned the other day when he was cleaning out the garage that he'd found some old pictures. They were of the past presidents and the club at a toy drive. It struck him as something they used to do that was for the community. The Bows had somehow lost touch with that. Leaving here in a giving mood, the men took the trucks, cars, and sidecar bikes to collect and distribute toys around our little slice of L.A. They wanted to be better...do better.

It was all about new beginnings and a new outlook now that Lucius had the reins.

I honestly think he's also trying to avoid the topic of his brother and Cap's whereabouts. Cap missing bothers him more than he's letting on. The playing card didn't sit well, and I can understand. I'd be off too. I still am. Anytime I look down the hall near the bathroom here at the clubhouse, it's a seedy reminder of death. A reminder of what

King, Scarlett, and Lucius' father did. The shit we've gone through is something no one should go through.

"Gazie, could you hand me that bowl?" I ask, smiling at the younger woman.

Handing over the bowl, I pour water into it. We're all making sure she's made to feel helpful, but used lightly. Gazie's no more than twenty-one, and has already seen more danger in this world than I have. Gazie had been stabbed by Munch's daughter. No one talks about the pyscho—it's as if she didn't even exist.

Even the nutty hang-around I had a run-in with when I first arrived hasn't been seen. I think it's a one strike you're out, no second chances. Just gone. The old ladies are a different story and a different breed. They're tough as nails and they take no shit. Taking a man's patch is a big deal.

"I can do more you know," Gazzie pipes in.

"We know. We're just not up for a moment of grumpy Munch," Carol says, touching Gazie's shoulder. "If you left here worn out, we'd never hear the end of it."

"I'm not a freakin' flower. I can do more than this," she argues, pulling the sling off her arm. "Colton can bite my ass if he thinks I'll be a trophy." Bending down, grabbing up a five-pound bag of carrots off the floor, she slings it up with a thump.

"No, you're not." Carol winks. "Munch may not know it, but he has his hands full with you, spitfire."

Picking up a peeler, I see her wince once, but she doesn't relent. I won't be the one to bother her about who's tough enough and who's not. As we set ourselves into a rhythm. With her setting the peeled carrots in front of me, and me cutting them, we finish pretty quickly.

"What did you buy the Pres for Christmas?" Helen asks me with a smirky grin. "I wasn't sure what to do for Miss. The club has been kinda dark for a few years, so this woohoo, tinsel, ho-ho-ho shit that you've brought here is bright. Miss is excited about something he bought, and

I'm not sure if what I got was good enough. We've never really done the exchange thing. I've just put a bow on before."

"The bow is an any day kind of gift. This is a step-up year. What did you get him, Hel?" Carol asks as she stirs the gravy while we turn her way.

With a straight face, she says, "A shirt."

A collective pause sets over us as we each turn to her.

I finally speak up, breaking the awkward silence, holding back the snicker that wants free. "I. um...I don't even know what to say to that."

"What's wrong with it? It's a nice T-shirt."

Letting the first giggle escape us, Carol collects herself with a tight smile. "I'm sorry. I wouldn't have thought of a shirt for Miss. A gun, a fletch of custom arrows, a new pair of riding boots—that's more Miss. That better be one fancy schmancy shirt."

"Is it wrapped? Can we see it?" Gazie asks.

She looks confused. "Why wrap it? He's just gonna put it on anyway," Hel huffs.

Putting down my knife, I wipe my hands on a dish towel. "Oh, now I need to see it."

"Fine. I'll go grab it." Helen washes her hands, dries them, then starts toward Miss's room in the compound.

The rest of us look at one another, wordlessly agree, and follow her like a pack of hungry dogs. Catching up to her at Miss's room, we enter as a gang, pushing our way in, grinning and giggling like idiots.

"Holy fuck!" I shout before covering my mouth with my hand. I've never been in here. I know I'm new, but after getting to know Miss a bit, I wouldn't have expected this at all. His room is stark, void of anything that would have you think he even knew what a bike was. One wall hosts a set of black and white framed pictures of vintage cars, while the other one holds a monster framed portrait of the actress from the *Vacation* movies. She looks amazing and perfect, sensual, and clearly homegrown. It's everything and nothing.

"He loves cars. Funny for a guy in a biker club, right? But that's him. That's why I got him the T-shirt." Bending down, grabbing a box out from under the bed, Helen opens it.

Holding it to her chest at first, afraid to turn it around, we all coax her with sweet prodding. Eventually she turns it. The white tee has a stark comment written right across the front in bold black letters.

I Like Big Blocks and I Cannot Lie, with a pair of pistons crossed over each other to look like tits. "See? He'll like it." Helen is proud of her accomplishment, and I won't be the one to burst her bubble. It is pretty perfect.

"I think it's funny." I smile and place a hand on hers. "He'll love it." I can't deny he won't because it's cute, funny, and super guy-like.

"I don't get it?" Gazie states.

Laughing collectively at the youngster in our group, we feel sorry for the youth of this world. "We'll explain it to you sometime." Carol starts out of the room, back toward the kitchen.

As we leave, Helen neatly boxes the shirt back up and hides it away again. "Do you think I should wrap it, Oubliette?"

Turning back from the doorway, I smile. "Nope. It's perfect, just as it is."

Chapter Eleven

Handing out toys for the past three hours has been one of those things that's made us all smile. Arriving at the community center, seeing the faces of the families and their children, downtrodden and miserable, I knew that my brothers and I had made the right decision.

Taking the remaining profits from the skin trade we had sitting in a dummy account—a business that we were now out of—paid for countless happy faces. Something that I never would've imagined saying about something so disgusting and evil. Human trafficking paid for these children's smiles. We're not those people anymore; we're not that club. *This* is who we are and who we will be.

The kids were fearful of us at first, and with good reason. We hadn't been approachable in the past, our dealings with the community was that of a heavy hand, and most of us were more gangster looking than nice. By the time we were done handing out presents and envelopes full of cash, though, we had children trying on cuts, asking for rides around the block, wearing helmets for pictures, and telling us their life stories. It was as good for them as it was for us.

We all needed the redemption and reflection of our goodness. We needed to be shown we were important and needed. That we would be better than we had been. One child in particular struck me deep.

Javier. Nine years old, tiny and malnourished, the boy still smiled even though it was easy to see his life was a struggle. His mother is an addict, desperate to find a release from a life she can't see hope in. They live on the streets, in a tent city that's torn down every week by city officials. She turns tricks to keep them alive. She can hardly care for herself, let alone his small life. The sisters that run this facility know who we are, and they know her well too. Javier has slept in the pews on the cooler nights.

Welfare is high in our area. Food stamps are a necessity, and gangs are prolific. All because we didn't step up. We allowed this to continue and to become as it is. We're still not the good guys, but we're here now, and we'll help out more than damage further.

I told his mom, Jasmyne, that Javier was welcome at the club anytime he wished. He loved the bikes, enjoying being told what different parts were. He soaked up the information like a sponge, and wished to be like me one day. I'm not sure I'm the material for a role model, but I was flattered.

Coming over to my side as I explain how the clutch works to Javier, Miss bends low to speak quietly in my ear. "Pres. I need your attention."

Tapping the youngster on the shoulder, I say, "Javier, go find Sister May. She's got pizza's coming in."

The look in his eye tells the tale—he's starved. Rising quickly, heading away, Javier practically runs to Sister May. Rising up, I come eye to eye with Miss. "Yeah. What's going on?" I ask.

"Your phone's been going off." Handing it to me, I see nine missed calls and three missed text messages.

"Thanks." Walking off to the side, I start scrolling through them. When we got here, all of us left our phones at the door. Respectful of the sisters and the church, we thought it was best to leave them until after we were about to leave. Eight of the calls are from Johnson. One I don't know. Seeing only one has a voicemail, I play it back.

"What the fuck are you mixed up in? I was contacted by the Federales this morning. I'm sitting down to...that doesn't matter. Anyway, they left me a message about tests done on a bottle and a cup. They were contacted by Interpol for the prints on it. The contents are what pisses me off the most. Who the fuck was messing with Colombians! Devil's Breath was in the bottle, Lucius. That shit would have you forgetting everything!" He pauses, then seeming to collect himself, he continues. "Lucius, someone's dealing with something really bad. The Queen would be the least of your troubles. Stay safe, stay out of shit over the holidays, and keep me in the loop."

"Well, fuck." That sucks. That explains why Cap doesn't remember anything about Maggie's death. Columbians, though? I don't remember pissing any off. Was one of those guys with King from the warehouse fight Colombian? That would make sense as to why Johnson thinks we're into something with them.

We don't need this shit. We're trying to go legit, or more legit than illegal, and the last thing we need is another fight on our hands.

Checking the texts next, one is a copy of the report sent by Johnson. One is Grady reminding me about dinner with Gem and Oubliette, and one has me falling to my knees.

Left to right.

Straight at night.

Your game ends with my might.

There's no player stronger than the Queen, Lucius.

You may have thought that taking the King ended the game, but I continue to play.

Queen to Pawn.

Stepping out of the church, walking around to the side, the text has an attached picture. Clicking the link, it opens a video. It's *the* video.

I hit play.

Within minutes, I see what I wished I didn't. It's Cap killing Maggie. I find it hard to watch, but I know there are clues that can help. With my stomach churning, and her death on his hands, I watch up to the ending. In the corner, someone directs Cap's moves. Their body is obscured behind the camera, but their voice is distinct.

I know who the mole in his club is.

It has me shaking as I set my phone away. Anger feeds my need to tear down those responsible. Walking back into the building, my anger dissipates slightly. It's Christmas, and the room full of children smiling from our good deed makes me feel better. But not enough.

"Miss!" He approaches me, leaving the coffee table where he was filling his face full of donuts.

"Pres?" The smile on his face disappears as he sees the fury coursing through me.

Laying down the last piece of his sparkly treat, I tell him, "Gather up. We have someplace to be."

"Just you and me, or the club?"

"Our hands are about to get dirty."

Smiling, Miss smacks the rest of the donut dust off his hands. "Oh, you know how to make a man happy."

He always knows how to make me smile in the toughest of situations. "Just get the boys. We have someplace to be."

Chapter Twelve

"**B**abe, I'm gonna be late. We might not be back for dinner. Something big came up." I called Obi while I'm waiting for the boys to round up and prepare to ride out. I knew she needed to know we'd be out late.

"Is it Cap?" Her voice is soft and disappointed but understanding.

"Yeah. I know who set him up. We're gonna pay them a visit. It's not gonna be pretty, Obi."

"Okay. I may not like it, but kick ass."

I snicker, but in a manly, of course. "I guess I'll kick some ass."

"Show them the side of you that I don't wish to be on the receiving end of. That asshole, kick ass, jerk side." Obi laughs.

Man, I'm glad I called her. "You know, you might've cooled me a bit, Obi. At least I won't go in opening fire without thought now."

"That's good."

"Someone *will* survive." Seeing the boys walk out, I can tell that their minds are on task. Miss must've given them a heads up. "Gotta go, love."

"Be home soon. I have a present for you."

Shit. Christmas.

"I'll be there soon. Promise," I tell her as I start my ride.

"I'll hold you to that." With that, Oubliette hangs up.

Pocketing my phone, I kick down the gear to first. "We have a bit of hunting," I tell Miss as he pulls his ride up beside me.

"Should I get my bow?" he asks with a devious smirk.

"No. That would be kind. Let's go hunt a rat."

Pulling out of the church parking lot, my mind reels with the destruction that's about to befall the man that crossed me and mine.

· · · ·

WITH THE SOUND OF OUR bikes rumbling down the street, it created a ruckus at their gates. Pulling up, the two men on guard try to seem intimidating. They're not. Revving my engine, allowing it to growl and snap, I don't bother shutting it down for the cunt on the left of me to speak. As he tries to ask questions over the noise, I ignore him. He's a prospect and not worth my time. The other jackass on the right, Joker, knows well enough not to piss me off.

Stepping up to my ride, I lock sights on him. Out of courtesy, I shut down my bike, but I don't order the others to do so. Their noise continues to cause a stir.

Setting my stand, lifting off the bike, I turn to him. "Jordan, this isn't the time to be balls to the wall. I need in that gate, I need Yeti, and if he doesn't come when I ask, I'll shoot every one of these motherfuckers." I point my Glock at his chest. "Even you, little brother. Even you."

I've known Joker for as long as I had Rap, and if Jordan thinks my brother's life is worth less than his or a man from his club, he's dead fucking wrong. Cap and I may not have been close in the past, but he's family, and I'll tear down the world for him.

"Lucius, I have no idea why you're charging up to the gates, guns drawn. It doesn't make sense. Care to tell me what's going on?" As a patched member of SoCal Soulless, I get it's his job, but this isn't the time for heroics.

"I know where Cap is. I *know* who sold him out. Who from your club did it. Maggie too." Now that I'm here and not talking to Obi, my adrenaline is revved back up and I'm ready to rain down hell.

The shock on his face is truthful. He didn't know. He raises his gun and clicks the safety. "Who? I'll kill the motherfucker myself."

"Step to the side, open the fucking gates, and I'll point you in the right fucking direction."

Joker looks to his prospect. "Open the gates, Boff."

Leaning a leg back over my bike, I start it up and wait for the gate to slide back. Resting my gun at my back, I start through to park at the doors. Yeti better be here, and he better be ready to tell me the fucking truth. I need answers, and I won't stop at his death to find out what I need.

With us riding through their gates, the residents of the clubhouse walk out. Some loaded with weapons, others, their demeanor does it for them. Cunty looking sons a bitches. Rag tag, young, old, war hardened and requiring their cuts hung up. They're a mess. No wonder the Queen went for Cap's boys.

"What the fuck is this?" One chimes off, cocking a sawed-off shotgun. "I'd like to know why a club's ridin' in unannounced when the Pres is out."

"The *Pres* is out because some motherfucker sold him out to the highest fucking bidder. Isn't that right, Yeti?" Turning to the prick, his stance is stern, proud, and without regret.

"I didn't do anything of the sort," he says smugly.

"Yeah?" I grind out every letter in the word. His attitude alone makes me want to put a bullet in his chest. Reaching in and taking out my phone, I turn up the volume and play the tail end of the video the Queen sent me.

"Make her bleed. It can't seem clean, Cap. She's being punished for her deeds." His voice over the tiny speaker floats on the dead air that surrounds us as we all listen intently. Those of his club turn to him with the same incredulous look as my men. They know what's gone on. I'm sure they helped remove Maggie's body. My men were oblivious, all but Miss. I appreciate though that they all stand by me as I go off on my own page.

Pocketing my phone again, I sneer at Yeti. "That was sent to me from the Queen, the cunt cartel bitch that you're working for." Stomping across the yard with my gun directed at his chest, I sneer, "You're gonna tell me where she is, where he is, and what the fuck's goin' on."

Standing his ground, squaring off against me, he still tries to seem tough. With his brothers looking to him, looking for answers, Yeti remains calm and silent.

"Nothing to say?" I shove my gun into his chest. "Nothing about where my brother is? *Your* brother that you swore to defend?" He still doesn't flinch.

Finally opening his mouth, every word that spills from his lips is vicious. "I do what's right."

Oh. "Is that so?"

"Yeah. That's so."

I close the distance between us, coming eye to eye with the fucker. "I can't believe you'd choose her over your brothers."

That's when I see the flinch in his gaze. Speaking low, he says, "I didn't choose *her*. I chose my *family*."

"She has someone of yours too?"

Pulling back, he looks me in the eye. "Yeah. And I want her back too."

As understanding settles within me, I holster my gun and motion for my boys to do the same. "I'd say we need a moment in your church alone, Yeti."

When I turn to Miss and the others, a strained calm returns to the group. One firecracker could set it all off. "I won't be long."

eaving with an understanding of Yeti's predicament, I realize how tough this is going to be. The Queen is far stronger than I expected.

Riding back to the clubhouse, pulling in just before seven with my stomach growling, the air surrounding the club is fresh and fragrant.

"Fuck, it smells great here." Flight licks his lips after stopping his ride in between Miss and Munch's.

"Better fuckin' believe I could eat the asshole out of a moose," Miss crows.

"Didn't you do that Tuesday?" Flight hops off his ride and out of range of the wide fist traveling his way.

"I dare your punk ass to call her that to her face, *Granger.*"

Flinching at the stab—Flight hates his real name—Miss laughs and starts off toward the clubhouse doors, seeming smug.

Yelling across the blacktop, Flight volleys back, "There's gonna be a day you'll need me, Miss. You'll need me, and I'll ask you what my name is. Then I'll walk the fuck away. Cunt!"

Raising a high middle finger to Flight, Miss's laughter can be heard even as he enters the building.

"So. The plan, Pres?" Flight asks.

"The plan is to not be killed by the girls. After all the planning they went through for tonight, we need to eat like Kings and say thank you. Then we'll worry about Cap and the Queen. Christmas Eve isn't the day to plan anything but full bellies and heads steamed up with beers. Tomorrow we'll work it out in church."

Nodding, he grins and tears off for the doors. "Good idea. I'm fuckin' starved, man."

That leaves Munch, Smart, Sinew, and me standing in the yard. Slowly making our way across the lot, I curse when my phone vibrates in my pocket. Knowing the only people who should be texting me are close, I don't look. I don't dare. I know there's only bad news.

"Fuck, I gotta go to the shop first and grab Obi's present. I'll see you in there in a sec, yeah?"

They nod, agree, and take off toward the food and booze.

Once they're gone I head into the garage, thankful it's empty and devoid of the twins. Passing through the space, past Diesel's nearly-completed ride, I turn the handle on the back room door. Obi's present is tucked away in there.

Pulling my phone out and reading the text, I remind myself that today is not the day. I blow out a stressful breath and pick up her present. I know she'll love it, but the moment is tainted with this newest disaster.

Yeti was wrong to do what he did, but I get it. I understand his need. I understand because here I am about to do the same thing. We'd trade anything to keep family safe. Even betraying all those that trust us to keep them safe too.

Chapter Fourteen

"**O**h my God, what took you so long!" Wrapping her arms around my neck, Obi rises on her tiptoes to kiss me. It's sweet, but commanding. I can't wait until she opens this gift. The head I'll get. An all access backstage pass to her and that ass I've waited for.

Though that's not my reason behind her present. Oubliette in a short time has pushed my envelope for so many things, and this is my way of thanking her. She's taught me to take life in stride. To be better.

She's made me *need* to make this club cleaner for those like her.

To be a better man.

Obi makes me enjoy the little things, and one of those things is Christmas. It was always a wasted time of year for me, and she's making me enjoy it for once.

I set her present on the floor. "We had to figure out a few things," I tell her as she steps back.

"Come on. You have to try this turkey. Helen is a fucking miracle worker with a stuffed bird." Grabbing my hand, she drags me across the space, past the makeshift dining areas. I tap some on the shoulder, smile, or acknowledge them as I pass. With full mouths, smiles in return, and 'Thanks, Pres,' it tells me that the girls did a great job. Even the tinsel doesn't seem overload after you fill the space with people and happiness.

"When did you get the tree?" I ask her. It's bright, thick, and every empty space surrounding it is covered with colorfully wrapped presents.

"I sent Fletch and Slam to pick one. I figured they couldn't do wrong." Looking at the tree and all the decorations on it, the tiny things seem out of place. Sweet, even.

"Obi?"

"Mm-hm," she responds slyly.

"When did you get a chance to string lights and shit while you were cooking and getting everything prepped?"

"It came that way. Nice, right?" Without skipping a beat, she hands me an empty plate. "Here. Eat."

"Obi. Where did the tree come from?" I see family photos and handmade ornaments. No way they came from here.

"They didn't say, I didn't ask. Now, go eat turkey." Leaving me to garnish my plate, she walks away, laughing.

Sneaky fucking woman. She fits here like a missing puzzle piece.

Wandering up to the table, smelling the food, seeing the bright dishes and the care put into them, puts a smile on my face. The last time I did this Christmas shit, I was a fucking kid. Removing the smile almost as quickly, I'm reminded that I also had Cap by my side. Setting the plate down and turning to the bar, I'm suddenly not hungry, or in a festive mood.

Quiver's standing there, waiting to hand me a whiskey. "You good, Pres? You look a bit off."

Sucking back the amber as fast as it had been poured, I reach out with the now empty cup to have it refilled.

I look over at Oubliette laughing, smiling, joking around with my family. "Not that she hasn't done a great job, but some wounds are too fuckin' deep, Quiv."

Pulling out his energy drink—seeing as how he doesn't do the liquor anymore—he swills a mouthful of his own. "I get ya' on that, brother. Do I ever."

"It just seems we're never catching a break. DG, True, Strike, the fights, then King, now with Cap." Sucking back the new glassful, I wince at the sweet burn. "Trying to go right, it seems to go all wrong."

"Did you think being president was a cake walk? Eyes open, brother. Eyes open. You can see the devil coming and think that you've won the war, but be ready for his army hiding in the wings. That's the real threat."

Choking on the mouthful I had, I laugh. "Even for a bartender, that's fuckin' deep, Quiver."

"I wasn't this deep before. That fancy fucking lady of yours has me goin' all philosophical and shit." I know what he says is true. "Don't mess that shit up, Pres. You won't only kick yourself, you'll wish we did too."

If he only knew. Setting my glass back on the bar, I stand, starting back to Oubliette. Most of the club has eaten, only those on the run still are, and they're settling around the tree with drink, family and laughter.

Eyeing me, Oubliette knows something's up. She's smart. That girl has a brilliant fucking mind. She can sniff out my lies. It'll take a lot out of me to be deceitful to her. Walking over, swaying her hips from side to side with a plate full of food, Obi narrows her eyes and smiles. "You didn't eat the turkey."

"I didn't have an appetite, babe."

"I call bullshit. Here." She holds up a fork laden with turkey and saucy gravy. "At least say you tried it so that Helen won't murder you in your sleep."

Dropping my guard and abiding by her request, I open my mouth as she slips it in. No use in arguing.

"Fuck," I mouth around it. "That shit's good."

"Told ya. Now here, eat." Shoving the plate into my hand, she smiles. "I'm going to help clean up, but when I come back, we're opening presents, mister."

"But—"

"No buts. Eat. I'll be back. The last thing you want to do is tell a tribe full of children that they need to wait longer because the president hasn't finished his veggies."

Fuck.

"Fine."

Chapter Fifteen

"**I** had to push him. I doubt he's eaten all day. I pretty much shoved the fork in his open yap." Washing dishes as Helen dries them, and Carol puts them all away, the children run around under our feet. Gazie, being closest in age, was in charge of shooing them out, entertaining them with tickles, candy cane bribery, and 'I'll tell your mom if you don't.'

With the rest away cleaning up the tables and settling our friends around the tree, I find a sense of peace doing something so mundane. The excitement of it isn't there, but I love it nonetheless. After the solitary life I've had—even with my brother by my side—this is the first time I feel a part of something. Included.

Picking up a pan to dry it, Hel laughs. "I handed a full plate to Miss as he walked in. I'm not sure if he inhaled."

"I inhaled," he says, shoving up behind her, grabbing her by the hips. "I'll show you how I can inhale you too." Tucking her in against him, Miss turns her chin to face him, kissing Hel deep. Pulling back, he whispers in her ear, "Hurry the fuck up. I'm hungry." Miss drags his hands up her waist, resting them on her breasts and squeezing. With a swift kiss on the cheek, pulling his arms back, smiling and wandering back out to the common area, he calls over his shoulder, "Ladies," in a smarmy tone.

Still holding the frying pan, Hel lifts it. "Keep walking Parker Jackson! Keep walking." Setting it on the counter with the stacked pans, she huffs, "Now I'm worked up. The audacity of him making me feel like that and walking away."

I laugh, because I know the feeling. "It's in their makeup. Tease, taunt, work us up, then they wait for us to come to them all needy and desperate for their touch." They want us twisted up in knots.

Bastards.

Setting the last clean dish on the counter, I dry my hands. "Anyone for a Dracula Fang? I feel we need something drastic to get through the next part."

With a round of "Hell yeahs" and "Why do you need to ask such a silly question," I leave the kitchen, heading for the bar. Reaching Quiver, I pass those already partaking in the revelry. "Move over old man. It's time for some magic."

Lifting his hands in defeat, he smiles and backs out of the bar. "I'll go grab a seat by the tree then."

"Good choice."

Behind the bar, lined up across the shelf, I grab up the nearly twelve bottles I need. Each in a specific order—mixed, shook, stirred and blended, I pour the concoctions into the highballs. Laying the final touch, a drip of crème de cacao, the ladies have all bellied up to the bar to watch what they call the *insanity train*. Placing one in front of each, they wait until I say go.

"All right. Grab 'em up, ladies."

Raising my own special crazy concoction, Carol chimes off a toast. "For the past we remember, for the present we enjoy, for the future we endure. Life is longer than one moment. Cheers."

"Cheers!" we all say in one voice, grinning like fools and laughing like school girls. Gathering our cups and heading to the tree, we sit surrounding it with our partners, lovers, friends, children, and families. Taking a seat on Lucius' lap—after he wouldn't let me sit beside him and insisted I sit on his knee—his arms curl around me. He dips a finger in my drink. "Mmm. That's fucking tasty. We may have to find other places to—"

"Children, Lucius. Children." I place a hand over his mouth and snicker. "Be good, just for a few minutes."

On his face is a fake, crestfallen look. "Fine. You have twenty minutes, tops."

"Twenty," I agree. "But. But...but, but, but...you need to say something to start this then."

"No."

"Yes," I state sweetly. "You can do it, Pres."

"I hate this."

"I had a feeling."

With a pinch on my ass, I squeal and jump up. The smile on his face tells me I'm in for a heap of trouble later, but I'll make him kiss my booboo better first.

Taking a seat on the chair he vacated, I wait.

Standing in front of everyone, he clears his throat. "Everyone. Thank you for a great time today."

The room settles, the guys get situated, and the kids quiet after a touch of prodding from the parents.

"I'm not good at this shit, but I guess it's just like Church. Chat, then drink beer, and find a bit of—"

"Busta!" I call out with a laugh.

He corrects his course. "Fine. Anyway, thanks. To the boys that joined me on the toy drive, it was great. To those who helped here," he looks at the twins, his face stating a conversation needed about the stolen tree, "nice tree. To the ladies that arranged some of the best fuckin' turkey I've ever had, it was great. So now, I hear we open presents." Letting out a heavy breath, he pauses for a second. "Most of you know my history, so let's say this is unfriendly territory and I'm glad I'm spending it with you. May the arrow strike true." He lifts his drink in toast.

"May the arrow strike true," the room replies.

Picking up a nearby present, he calls out, "Nordstrom!" The small boy wanders up with glee in his eyes. Taking the present, Lucius calls out the next, one by one, until they've all rushed up. "Marnee, Castiel, Rochelle and Avrille." Once each kid has a wrapped package in their hands, torn apart and joy in their eyes, the adults wait their turn.

They all say their 'thanks' and run off to enjoy their spoils. That leaves us.

Picking up the box that we'd finally enticed Helen to wrap up, she hands it to Miss. Pulling off the paper with disregard, he smiles when the box shows his reward. "That's the shit, lady!"

Grinning, Miss yanks her to his waist and smacks her ass as he reaches behind his chair. "Your turn now." He lays a box on the floor in front of her. Flipping it open, she squeals.

"No fucking way! No way! Really? You're kidding, Colton! You're kidding, right?"

"If I didn't mean it, do you think I'd give it to you?"

Wrapping her arms around his neck, she hops up on his lap and swings her legs around his waist. She's ecstatic.

"Are we missing something?" Carol asks.

Shrugging his shoulders, he smacks Helen's ass. "I gave her my patch...if she wants it."

"Of course I want it!" Kissing him hard on the mouth, their hot and heavy noises kick up a notch.

"Take it back to your room," Carol comments.

"Or strip her down. Let's watch," Quiver jokes. At least I hope he's joking.

"No head for you, Quiv," Miss laughs. "But for me there is. Night, boys." Lifting Helen, the two of them head off like giddy kids.

Running down the rest of the gifts, the men hand them out to their girls, the girls to their guys, and the adults quickly dissipate from the room, leaving only a few of us behind. Lucius walks over to the door and picks up a gift wrapped in newspaper, then lays it at my feet. "It's heavy, Obi."

"Okay." Peeling back the newspaper, at first, I'm not sure why he's giving me bike parts, then I see the taps. "Are these handlebar beer taps?"

Leaning against the wall, he watches as I tear it apart. "Yeah, babe. I thought you'd like something custom."

"They're so fucking cool." They're heavy, like he said, but they're totally neat. "I can't wait until we hook them up."

"Quiv' might be pissed off if you do it here, but if you want them at Humble, I've already talked to Death. He'll help me install them after the holidays."

Fantastic. It's truly amazing how he thought to do something so nice for me. Now to give him his gift. This is going to throw him off.

Hopping up off the chair, I walk to the tree and grab the envelope. Handing it to him, I take a seat once more.

Chapter Sixteen

The thin white envelope sits in my hands. I tore it open to look at a card that honestly makes no sense. On the front is a pair of yellow children's characters with a saying, *Bannana!*

Confused, I look to Oubliette.

"Open it, Lucius," she coos, as cool as a cucumber. Something is definitely up.

"It's not going to explode or anything?" I query.

"Nope. But you might."

Still wondering what she means, knowing I'm fucking tired after today and all that's gone down with Cap's club, it actually deters me from opening it. "I can't take more surprises today, babe. Can we just go to bed? I want to fuck you."

"Open it, pussy."

"Fine," I growl, flipping open the cover. I stare at the words written in black and white. I'm not sure if my day became better or harder.

"Weren't you drinking all day?" I ask, slightly annoyed, but I try to hold it back.

Standing from the chair, she giggles. "I'm a chemical genius and a bartender. I can whip up the best non-alcoholic drinks you can imagine."

I don't know what to say. Nothing I say right now would be good. Not after that text earlier.

Saying nothing and heading for the door, I walk out.

Rushing out behind me, she yells, "That's it? Nothing to say?"

Making my way to my bike, I straddle the seat. "I can't say much right now. I have to go, Oubliette." Turning the key, I start it up and say nothing else.

Seeing the sadness in her eyes through my rearview mirror breaks me. I turn the curb and don't look back. I can't. If I do anything more than I already have, I'll not only be putting her life in danger, but that of our unborn child.

Nothing has changed. Christmas is a fucking curse.

Merry Fucking Christmas to me.

I really wish the Queen hadn't sent me a picture of Oubliette today with the words:

We know your weakness.

You took my family from me, so I took one of yours.

Come to me or I'll take all you hold dear.

You have twenty-four hours, Lucius, to be at the coordinates.

Follow the rules of the game.

Q

Driving off, I can't see another way out of this. I do now what I must. What I have to, to save them all.

Don't miss out!

Visit the website below and you can sign up to receive emails whenever Kerri Ann publishes a new book. There's no charge and no obligation.

https://books2read.com/r/B-A-SLJG-ELMAB

BOOKS 2 READ

Connecting independent readers to independent writers.

Also by Kerri Ann

Broken Bows, SoCal Soulless MC
Queen
Knight

The Broken Bows
Rook
King
Pawn
Gambit
Bishop's Play

Watch for more at https://www.authorkerriann.com.